Lost Crusaders of Leadership

The Untrained Unchecked & Unprocessed

Apostle Natasha Jennings

The Lost Crusaders of Leadership

Copyright © 2022 Apostle Natasha Jennings

Cover Design by: Lady Marketing Group

Orders by U.S. trade bookstores and wholesalers.

ISBN-13: 9798849510576

Printed in the United States of America

Acknowledgement

To the father who gives me strength and gives me songs

of deliverance, may the gift that you've given me be a

help and a footstool to someone…somewhere

Table of Contents

What is it?

Regardless of what, why and where you lead, you -- as the leader -- are directly responsible for the engagement of those who follow you.

Whether you're leading a family, a class or a corporation, leadership means inspiring others to achieve certain outcomes, and it's up to you to decide whether you are leading positively or negatively -- and whether you choose to focus on engagement or merely output. Leadership can often be equal parts high confidence and self-esteem and worrying if you're doing it right while continually searching for answers. Whether you're a leader in an organizational setting or have high influence in some other capacity, improving your leadership begins with a *focus on improving what you're already good at.*

We would call that leading with your strengths: the things that come naturally to you and that help you succeed daily. When you intentionally apply your strengths as a leader, that's when your life and the lives of those you lead begin to change.

This book will provide you with new ways to think about your role or position as a leader. Legitimate improvement begins with a refusal to ascribe to one-size-fits-all solutions. You will discover why your strengths matter and then learn to use yours to become a transformational leader. You the reader will be reading about the most dangerous leaders in ministry and how to spot them and how to disarm them and deal with the spirit behind it. These "Lost Crusaders" cause severe damage in a ministry. I have seen it happen. So stay open and prayerful about being the leader that God has called you to be as you begin to read.

Leadership definition, in its simplest form, means "the act of getting individuals aligned and moving in the same direction toward a desired outcome."

Effective leadership has a lot to do with inspiring, aligning and then activating -- but it doesn't end there. A key to effective leadership is the ability to define outcomes, but then helps individuals put their talents to use to get there. The best leaders know their people and are more aware of those people's strengths than they are of their weaknesses. Great leaders aren't blind to their own or others' weaknesses; they just know that their competitive edge lies within their strengths.

Having clear expectations in your role as a leader is vital to success. Most of the time, understanding your role and the expectations that come with it begins with deciding what outcomes or goals need to be met. Whether you define them yourself or have an organization define them for you, they need to be clear, manageable and well-communicated. When leaders lack clear expectations for their own roles and outcomes, it can create a lack of trust among their followers. They can come off as incompetent and lose buy-in from their team members.

What makes a good leader?

A good leader takes responsibility for their leadership. They understand that everything they do directly affects the people they lead. In other words, the best leaders lead with their followers in mind. I've studied which leadership skills are the most important to a follower. What do you think we found? Maybe "good communication," "motivational" or "highly committed"?

While these traits are certainly important for leaders, what followers crave the most are trust, compassion, stability and hope. Let's talk about traits that make a leader great.

Trust: Building trust is the foundation for leading. Honesty, clarity and behavioral predictability all make up trust. Leaders must adopt the trait of trustworthiness and prioritize it as one of their most important skills -- because without it, people won't feel as confident to follow. *Example:* Share your concerns or struggles as a leader. By modeling this, your followers will be more likely to trust you with theirs.

Compassion Bring positive energy and a willingness to listen. Being compassionate means caring about your followers holistically while seeing them as more than just their ability to perform. Compassionate leaders should be willing to share their own struggles and accept the same honesty from others. *Example:* React calmly and empathetically when followers are dealing with difficult situations in work or life. From family burdens to workplace burnout, modeling compassion can help them succeed.

Stability Ensure people can count on you. Providing stability looks like creating space where people feel psychologically safe, like they can depend on you to answer their questions, hear their ideas and address their concerns. Communication is key for this trait. Stability puts emphasis on the current moment, keeping people grounded in the here and now -- knowing they can count on you. *Example:* Try to be as consistent as you can when responding to those who follow you. Seek to answer the questions your followers have. This will help provide the stability they crave.

Hope: Encourage people to believe in a better future. While stability focuses on today, hopefulness deals with the future. People need to see that their leaders have a clear direction in mind. They want to have faith that their leaders are guiding them in the right direction. When leaders communicate hope, they can help followers feel more enthusiastic about the future. *Example:* Talk about the future as if it's bright. Even when things are hard, you can acknowledge difficulties while still communicating the best possible outcome to your followers.

To practically apply these traits, make them a part of your everyday communication. Every email, conversation, instruction, etc., should be building hope, trust, stability and compassion. Executing them every day will make them more easily become a part of you.

The 7 things well

What *all* leaders need is a fresh look at the leadership

behaviors that actually contribute to performance,

development and success.

These are the expectations for every leader:

- Build relationships.

- Develop people.

- Lead change.

- Inspire others.

- Think critically.

- Communicate clearly.

- Create accountability.

These expectations work in any scenario where there's a leader. No, really -- think about it. CEOs? For sure. Professors or teachers? Definitely. The leader of your small group at church or facilitator of a book club? No doubt.

Being able to do these seven things well can be the biggest differentiator between being an average leader and an exceptional leader.

- **Build relationships**. The concept of "leadership" cannot exist apart from a group of people who need to be led. Simply put, leaders can't lead unless someone follows, which means that building strong relationships is key. People need to connect with each other, share trust and have relationships to thrive. It is important to recognize the value of people, seek to know them for who they are and build lasting connections.

- **Develop people.** Do the people you're leading, coaching, teaching, etc., feel like they're growing? Most people know that if they're not growing, they're not getting closer to success. Then, it's only a matter of time before they leave -- your organization, your fitness class, your night class -- for someone who gets them closer to their goals. Every day, those people have a chance to either get a little bit better at what they do, or not. development can, and should, be constant.

- **Lead change**. The keyword being "lead." Much is expected of you as a leader to keep moving forward, ensuring that the purpose, mission and vision remain the same. It's OK (and good) for you to charge your followers with some responsibility for change -- coming up with good ideas, better ways of doing things or smarter processes -- because it will help them take ownership for helping with the right kind of change. Every individual is able to see an opportunity and take initiative, set a goal and create a plan to get there, but it's your job to set an example for that.

- **Inspire others**. Is this trait too "soft" to count as an expectation that's critical to success? Definitely not. Leaders should provide inspiration so that others can find greater meaning in a vision or purpose. Without meaning, and without connecting inspiration to the individuals who follow you, you'll find that those who follow will have a difficult time committing themselves to the greater purpose -- whether that's in your organization, classroom, small group or otherwise. This expectation helps people see that every little thing they do matters.
- **Think critically**. Aimless decision-making and feeble thinking have no place

in leadership. Or, at least, they shouldn't be the type of thinking that influences final decisions. Evaluating plans, understanding risk, organizing thoughts and creating action steps requires leaders to bring their whole selves and think critically. Success requires establishing an aim and devising a comprehensive, multifaceted approach to achieving it.

- **Communicate clearly**. Learn the best way you communicate, and then learn how others like you to communicate with them. Share information and ideas that matter -- because effective communication means you'll need to convey compelling information that leads to more informed actions and decision-making. Don't think of communication just as telling your followers things, but think of it as sharing information, asking questions, listening and brainstorming. These are all important forms of clear communication in leadership.

- **Create accountability**. Every person is accountable for something. But this is especially true for leaders. Responsibility is expected of you, just as much as it is of those who follow you. You expect the students at your fitness class to bring the right equipment; you expect that your employees are held accountable for their deadlines, and so on. A culture of accountability starts with you. In practice, this may look like openly committing to initiatives, plans or ideas so that everyone knows what you're responsible for. It may also look like you apologizing to those you lead when you drop the ball in a significant way. Accountability creates a better environment for your followers and allows them opportunities to become more efficient and creative through their own responsibilities.

What's my leadership style?

There are countless ways you could answer this question. But most people look to academic leadership theories or find a list of leadership personality traits and different leadership styles to try to answer this.

For example, there's transformational leadership or authentic leadership. *Well, wait, aren't all leaders supposed to be these two things?* Then there's transactional leadership and laissez-faire leadership, or you could be more autocratic or a coaching leader. *OK, now I'm really confused.*

With many ways to pinpoint your leadership styles or categorize your relationships with your followers, your attempts may leave you feeling discouraged or irritated. But if you're not sure what kind of leader you are, how are you supposed to find support or improve?

Most leadership categories are all about how a person behaves when they're leading a group -- when really, you should be focusing on the things that you already know and that are easier to identify: your natural patterns of excellence. These natural strengths tell you more about why you lead the way you do and how you lead best than about what kind of leader you are.

Maybe something you're naturally drawn to as a leader is being vocal and being someone who is always in front of the room. This could be your Communication theme .Influencing: Or maybe you find yourself being the leader who is always pushing their team to go further, reach higher and continually challenge themselves. This could be your Achiever theme. Executing, could you be the leader who is energized by brainstorming sessions and who loves thinking about all the things that could be? This could be your Ideation theme. Strategic Thinking

Or maybe you're the type of leader who listens to everyone's individual story and sees the unique value that every follower brings to your team. This could be your Individualization theme. Relationship Building

Successful Teamwork

A successful team is a team where individuals are positioned to do what they do best and get the resources and partnerships they need to do their best work. Leading a successful team requires you to identify the unique contributions that every person on your team makes -- including yourself. To lead a successful team, be willing to admit to your team that you're not great at everything. It's good to acknowledge, and it's even better for your team to hear.

Conventional wisdom says that to become a better leader, you should develop the areas where you are naturally weak. And to be a good leader, you encourage your team to do the same; you should invest in the places where you're naturally strong.

Unchecked, Untrained & Unprocessed

To relate to those who follow you, you must first learn to follow. There are so many examples of what not to do in the bible that can cause disruption for the person you follow. Yes, even as a follower in leadership you can cause a disruption that will take the focus off Christ and the leader who is trying to lead the sheep. I did not intend to want to go through these points but I feel as if I must because I am beginning to see more and more of these destructive behaviors across the board.

UNCHECKED

A leader with a "superiority complex" mind causes disruption. This mindset leads to the leader thinking that the job of the Shepherd he or she can do it better or, it's just not in the way that they believe it should go, so this person will use the word for their own selfish gain to prove a point, or let me say it this way, a sense of one's own importance or abilities.

This inferiority complex is fastened in poor self-esteem and resistance when asked to perform a job function which they believe is beneath them, which brings them to resisting any authority, and this causes them to discuss with others who are following them, or who they have influence over to get them on their bandwagon and to agree with how they feel, and use scripture totally out of content to make a point. This is DANGEROUS and it flows from a spirit of rebellion. I can't tell you how many times I have seen this destructive behavior and it never ends wells, only in the person leaving a ministry unchecked, going from house to house unable to grow and get correction, and gathering nonbelievers and even some saints who don't know the difference in disobedience or rebellion. This person likes to give the "scoop" on a certain ministries and leaders that they refused to submit and commit to, so they begin a campaign of running the work of the Kingdom down and these unfortunate weak-minded souls end up more confused and lost than ever before that are influenced by them. A servant leader that wrestles with obedience is a cause for alarm. As a servant leader, instruction in your growth process is vital to a growing spiritual life.

UNPROCESSED:

The Shepherd which not only acts as your leader
but as a mentor also will instruct you in matters
that will not only become difficult but
instructions that will challenge you and yet at
the same time pull out those things (gifting's)
out in your spirit that serves you later down the
line. Often the mistakes that we make are
sometimes common mistakes. The main
common mistake is listening to others tell us our
time is "NOW" only to step out into the deep
prematurely, to find out that we are not good
swimmers as we think we are, and if we had
waited we could have not only went much

further, we could have had some help, TIMING IS EVERYTHING! A servant leader who demands order in the church but has no order in their life, can tell you what the order is in ministry and every function of the gospel, but home life and or marriage is one of complete turmoil. Every Shepherd should know how their leaders are living, now I didn't' say go into their home and regulate their every move, when they will eat dinner, how they discipline their children, that is truly stepping over the boundary line. How they live is the job of the Holy Spirit to correct, but you should at least counsel your leaders to make sure that they are well in their life, marriage, children, financial etc. As a servant leader in any capacity you must understand that there is no way that you can lead others where you have not been, especially since there is so much at stake. God forgive us all for the countless mistakes we have made concerning people.

A leader's job is sometimes a thankless job, but there are so many bright sides to this amazing responsibility that are too numerous to begin to name. Firstly, do you realize that you are helping your leader to equip the saints for the work of the ministry? You lift the vision of the house up (not your vision) You speak what your leader is speaking as he/she hears from Christ. You have an amazing responsibility to impact the lives of others through Christ in such a way that the very words that Christ allows to flow through you are what they may need in the next dimension of their life in ministry! and after they have gotten what it is they have need of, here comes the hard part and good part. I'm not speaking of the many conversations of helping couples stay together; not praying for the children and watching them grow, weddings or funerals or even ordinations all of that is great, I'm speaking of releasing them Him/her to do the work of the ministry, watching the people of God function in what the Lord has given them to do for the building of the Kingdom. We must disciple! This is a mandate that we teach others to pray, to travail, to love others, to listen for the voice of the Lord. How to gird yourself through the word. Faith! What we believe. This nugget is for the Senior leader, but you defiantly can be

blessed by it also. This soul that you have helped

nourished under your head leader and showed

love and compassion too for many years, when

it's time for the release it can be the hardest

thing that you must do.

LETTING GO

The other flip side of this is when you are the Senior Shepherd you must let others go who feel they have outgrown you and the ministry and you know this is not so. What do you do? when this painful staff departure is not only sudden but you know right now it's not a good move? Certainly, you can talk with them about it, but how effective would it be if they know that it was a "God said" thing. Well you first must realize that we all grow at different rates and if they choose to "go" instead of "grow" you must be as kind and gracious to let them go, just as you were when you received them into the fold. Why put up a fight? When this is what they have desired to do. Trust me; this has been brewing for quite some time. You noticed when they started pushing back of the normal routine things that they were doing in the church or ministry, it's ok, only deal with the departure as far as their influence reach.

There is a difference between church business and member business, if it is not necessary to publicly release the departure than don't. Your job is to keep the sheep safe always. I tell you I deal with this common issue a lot when I do seminars or leadership learning sessions, it's very important how this is handled and yes this is compassion, because it still must be done and handled in love and with respect.

UNTRAINED

Staying focused and executing the will of the father must be the object of movement in the kingdom. It's important to know the will of God for the effectiveness to be adequate for the necessary growth and victory of those that you are helping.

Whether you're sitting under a leader or have your own ministry that you are the Under Shepherd, knowing the will of the father is so important. He makes us all different with different callings so it's very important to establish and know just what your niche is and what the giftings are in you.

It's important that we understand those gifting's and make sure that we exercise in them, so they become stronger and we are more experienced in them. So, if you know you have the gift to sing why not work on perfecting that gift by investing in music tracks, a vocal coach, getting in the choir. Why do we believe that God gives us a gift and we don't need to exercise it? If you have the gifts of prophecy why not connect to a prophet that has been walking in this office for many years and has perfected this gift. We cannot take the attitude that we know what we are doing without the proper training and seek to "Try it out" on the members on a Sunday because you have chills that you believe is the Holy Spirit and you must get this word out now!

How can you know the ins and outs of the gift if you don't get training in that gift from someone who has mastered it and can help guide you and help you become effective in it, after all it is for the kingdom. If you look at your gifting as a true blessing you will know and understand that the training can possibly help make someone's journey a little bit better, help make them go a little further and do major damage in the enemy's camp. Please get training so as not to cause a train wreck in the marketplace or in the church. Souls need what you have. Invest, train and be great in it.

It's important to invest in yourself and attend local or regional training forums with those who have walked where you are walking. There is nothing wrong with reading books like this one that will help you to understand and learn new and different techniques to help you become more effective in your calling. The Bible tells us to make our election sure. Train in that thing, ask questions about what you don't understand, this is just not more training so that you can show your leader or church what you can do, this is about you taking active participation in your life to the call that you believe you have been chosen too, take this advice from me, if you cease to learn you cease to grow.

It's important that you never forget that you must keep growing and keep learning you will never know it all; there is no resting place where you have nothing else to learn.

Relational Competence

Relational Competence can be described as living in relation to others or interconnecting with others with a common goal in mind. Having relationships that are critical to developing short-term and long-term goals. Not only is this type of relationship necessary for ministry it is necessary for your own personal growth. Meaning this formula for relationships can be used both ways. There is no way to be successful in ministry or even in the corporate world without a good team. You cannot win without a good team, it is imperative that you have a group of people who will not tell you whatever you want to hear, because they want to be a part of the group, which creates a deficient. You always want people who surround you with a positive mindset and the wiliness to get the job done with a willing humble and faithful attitude. Why is this so important? There is nothing that has a division in it that will stand very long. To reach a common goal there must be clear thinking of who and what the vision and visionary is, everyone is given their lane and when choosing the right team, it helps the leaders to cover their lane and be successful in it which can cause a growth spurt in your team members, which after all your reproducing what you are right?

A good leader always trains someone to take their place that's why you continuously develop and reproduce yourself in the likeness of Christ. God told Moses he would put his spirit (Moses) on the elders (leaders), why? Because Moses already had God's spirit: *Numbers 11:17 And I will come down and talk with thee there: and I will take of the spirit which is upon thee, and will put it upon them; and they shall bear the burden of the people with thee, that thou bear it not thyself alone.* God told Moses to get 70 elders (leaders) of the people and officers over them, and he would take the spirit in Moses and put it on them. Do you realize what the most critical relational competence component is?

Listening… Yes, this word is critical to

everything. Most people (especially those who love to hear themselves talk) fight being obedient, most never move in the direction that God has for them for several reasons. This is truly a spirit that causes people to miss out on what God has for them.

- **They are not humble**
- **An "I am right attitude"**
- **Listening to respond.**

I believe out of all three critical directional crashes that can cause a servant leader to miss out on valuable information and direction. Let's pull one that trips leaders up the most. Listening to respond. This is the most non-thinking critical relational competence of them all…

Why? Because the knowledge or information that is being given out at that time, tends to get lost in the need of the person to identify that what they are saying is more important than the information that is being handed to them, so instead of listening to understand, an irrational answer is given because of the need to be heard, not to understand. We all need understanding in our dealings with one another, but in leadership it's important that we listen to understand if we are to help the other person come to a decision of salvation or deliverance.

We sometimes present the cure without the person knowing they are sick.

When approached with this mindset years ago, I was slightly taken aback, to the responsive answers that sounded as if they were using an antidote for the wrong disease. This type of mindset with the other components listed above can do more damage to a leader and leadership itself. It's important that we "Check ourselves" and what we offer, because could it be there may be a hindrance that we are unaware of that causes a stumbling block for others. As leaders it's important that God gets all the Glory from what we do. I often go into churches or corporate venues when asked to do what they call a "Learning Observation" or "Self-Check" about what can be done better among the leadership or team to make the interaction with one another more effective so that production can be at an all-time high, or in other words what can be changed or improved upon. There have been lots of things that I have noticed and something's that have been great and some things that have been not so great in ministry areas.

Listed below is not the end all list of everything but they are things that have come up repeatedly.

Observations of Learning: Sitting in counseling sessions with other leaders: When a leader must be corrected or given advice it is not uncommon for a Pastor or CEO to do, after all that is the job to grow great leaders.

- To spare you is to spoil you. There is no way you can ever be great without correction and criticism it grows the most venerable part of you.

- Servant leaders are always the team cheerleaders encouraging others to go and do their best and move toward their destiny and to be all God has called them to be.

- Time conscience being on time says a lot about you and the God you serve. I will never understand how people can make it to their employment on time, but show up late for ministry duties. Priorities have got to be in place. Remember, how you follow is just as important as how you lead. You should never show up on time ONLY when you are on the program to do something, after all aren't we living epistles? our lives are showcased to others as examples of Christ. People look to us for guidance. How can we ask of others what we don't do ourselves?

- Giving Consistency, far be it from me to get into a debate about the Old & New testament concerning tithing (that is not what this statement is about) however I will say this, the church is a nonprofit, how can you watch the house fall under your leadership, and bills go unpaid under you? If every leader looked like you, what would your ministry look like? Be the example that you would want others to follow.

- Purpose as a leader you should know what your purpose is, why you are there in that organization, this will help define your future.

- Authenticity, the worst thing you can do is emulate your leader. It's too hard trying to be someone else, you are more effective when you truly comfortable being you

Again, relational competence does play a great deal of importance when dealing with others. Why is this so important you ask? Because we are in the "people" business! Everything that we do affect someone be it good or bad. We as leaders and myself included, must understand that people come from all walks of life and experience different things, some I could not even phantom to have gone through, some are survivors, some are simply surviving, but it's our job to help them receive the deliverance and the healing that God has available for them.

Back to why I even talked about my Observations of Learning. Firstly, I thank God for my leader who allowed me to sit in on meetings, and training when I was becoming a young minister in the church. Seeing the actual behind the scenes, all the ends and outs and all the many decisions that must be made so that the vision can stay in the forefront. It really takes work. If every leader where to just give the sheep a glimpse of the many counseling sessions, marriage engagement sessions and the little small foxes(problems) that arise on a day by day moment. I'm convinced folks would really be disciplined in their prayer life. *Galatians 5:13 For, brethren, ye have been called unto liberty; only use not liberty for an occasion to the flesh, but by love serve one another.* Paul tells how we should serve, not in flesh because it profits us nothing, in its dwells no good thing so why would we become wrapped up in it trying to serve in the flesh. It becomes messy, if someone doesn't react the way we think they should, we become offended because out motives have now become tainted or cloudy so to speak and if we serve in the authentic way that the scripture tells with humbleness and love, we don't run the risk of being in offense and strife

We are not giving this long contract of do's and don'ts that would take a lawyer and a magnifying glass to read. Just humbleness and love would really take us a long way. When speaking of Christians everywhere are called to serve one another, It is not a special request, this part of the Christian lifestyle and Jesus expects us to do it in such a way that he gets the glory and the person that we are serving is blessed. Check your spirit next time you find yourself in a position that you are serving, ask yourself is this what God wants? am I humbling myself in love so that God can be glorified? is he really pleased with my attitude? or am I moving in flesh to satisfy some need or issue that has not been surrendered to Christ? When people have a distrust or disappointment in their leader, they are questioning their character whether they know it or not. that is what is happening. A servant leader it is your duty to undergird your leader, and show him/her in a positive light, even if you know their struggle. and whatever may be happening in his life. Your job is to pray for them and keep them lifted, not slander and gossip about them, this breeds contempt and division, and you will certainly answer to the Lord for it. *1Corinthians 1:10-13 Now I exhort you brethren, by the name of our Lord Jesus*

Christ, that you all agree and that there be no divisions among you, but that you be made complete in the same mind and in the same judgment. It's easy to see the faults in your leader, because we put their life and every word under a microscope, and forget that they are not exempt from mistakes and even putting their foot in their mouth. It is only because they are out in the forefront that the spotlight is always shining, but as we talked before, the role of the servant leader is one to uplift. You are called in the capacity that you are in to help them help others. You just read about Moses in the paragraphs beforehand. The Shepherd cannot do it alone, they need the help of the servant leader which consists of Deacons, Ministers, Elders, etc. and other secondary servant leaders who help to address and work with the sheep. In other words, the servant leaders help to bridge the gap between the sheep and the shepherd. This is very important; again I say this one person can't do it all.

Usurp/Presumptuous: These two destructors have no place in the servant leader's movement in the Kingdom; they bring damage and can spread like a cancer. Every Under shepherd will tell you that these culprits are the main cause of situations, misunderstandings and total out of order servant leaders. Sometimes unknowing and I would like to think that way and that it would not be done on purpose. Let's look at them shall we. I will end this chapter with the definition from Webster's so that we have an understanding.

Usurp, *takes a position of power or importance illegally or by force.* **Presumption**, *a person that exhibits a behavior by failing to observe the limits of what is permitted or appropriate.*

PRESUMPTION

Moving in a presumption in ministry is costly, especially when you're giving out advice, not that you can't, however it's important in secondary leadership that you pay attention and know what is being asked of you, so that you don't interfere with what Christ is doing.

I've seen this often too many times. There's nothing wrong with waiting to talk to others on the team, because you can get tricked into giving an answer that did not even deserve a reply, and you will be held accountable for the reply that you gave. Words can be wrong or just out of season, as a servant leader please let me offer you this advice, it's important to interact with sheep with another servant leader with you when giving a reply. This covers you and the person whom you're giving the reply to. The Under Shepherd at most times has foreknowledge of a situation, in other words they may know facts that you don't, why give your advice or two cents on a situation that you clearly know they are being counseled for. See the definition: *failing to observe the limits of what is permitted or appropriate.*

When you are in the secondary leadership position or servant leader it's important to understand that it's ok to say, "I don't know" or "I don't have the answer for that" We sometimes have this face or front to put on to make others believe that we know the answer to their problem, when we do not. Servant leader understand this, we do not have an answer for everyone who comes to us, and while it's very dangerous we sometimes move in the job of the Holy Spirit. Instead of others seeking the answer in prayer they begin to come to us for major decisions instead of Christ. The best advice is to say, "I may not know the answer, but you know what let's pray about it, let's see what Christ says about it. Let's find out his heart for this thing you are seeking answers for." Also, I'm going to make a brief statement about presumption when at the altar. The altar call is a time when saved and unsaved alike come to the altar during an open Sunday service for whatever the reason, prayer for a situation or sickness or to give their life to Christ, whatever the reason, this is not the time for you to show what your gifts can do, or to show that you are called in your title and it's now your time to shine. No! again that is not what this time is for.

Some come to the altar for unanswered questions from God not you, most come because they have been beaten down all week from family, life situations and marriage disputes, sickness etc. and desire prayer, there are many reasons and some come to give their life to Christ. This is not the time for you to fail to know the limits of what the Under Shepherd has set in this church. This is not about you! It's great if your gift helps someone, but remember you have a set leader and if the leader states he will pray a prayer over all without laying hands, it's not the time for you to lay hands and take the altar over.

We must obey and follow instructions. The presumption spirit will cause you to move completely out of order making you delusional of the mistake that your making if the Lord is giving directions to the leader, you must obey and follow as not to cause a train wreck to an innocent soul that is seeking the face of God. Stay in your lane! That is the best advice that I could possibly give you, so that presumption spirit doesn't take over and understand this, the Bible tells us that everything lawful is not always expedient. (1 Corinthians 10:23) In other words, just because you can doesn't mean that you should. Let's be mindful that we always want to do our best so that God can get the glory in all that we do.

USURP

Now let's discuss the usurp spirit, normally when you are speaking of this diabolical action, yes, I know the strong word but it takes strong maneuverings for this unchecked spirit to move and allow things to happen.

The overthrow so to speak or illegally take a position that was not purposed for you. This usurp spirit happens when truly the person thinks more of themselves they ought Paul says in *Romans 12:3 "Do not think of yourself more highly than you ought, but rather think of yourself with sober judgment"* I'm convinced that when we begin to seek that which is not intended for us, we would have begun this downward spiral of needing to be seen and it's what I call "glory junkies" or "glory zombies" A person conscious is seared to the things that make them alive, filled with joy and of the fruits of the spirit. This spirit is of the devil because it comes from him. When Lucifer decided that he wanted the glory of God. *Isaiah 14:13 For thou hast said in thine heart, I will ascend into heaven, I will exalt my throne above the stars of God: I will sit also upon the mount of the congregation, in the sides of the north:...*This spirit of usurp makes you think that you are qualified for a position that you have no understanding or training in, or you are more important than the person who is set in place, this is not just the Under shepherds office, this is an office normally where this person can be seen by others to get attention or praise or pat on the back. A glory junkie feels they deserve to be glorified, instead of staying humble and rather as the scripture says to think of yourself with sober judgment, what does that mean? Sober judgment, a judgment of oneself that is free of exaggeration, it's almost as if the person is moving with a Napoleon complex. They think that they are bigger than they really are. You will find an example of this in small dogs. They bark continuously and they appear ferocious, but upon looking at them you realize they are all bark and no bite. Just an animal that is so small with big aspirations to make you think they are bigger than not only you, but the world. Now I could go on and on about the Usurp authority, but I will end it here. It is a very mean and unproductive way to get what you're after.

If your desire is what God desires than you will have what's for you, no longer can we allow this spirit to run rampant and push its way through meaningful ministry while causing collateral damage to others in the process. It must go and it cannot under any circumstances be tolerated. The damage that is caused is mortifying, there is nothing more tiresome than to witness this spirit allow themselves to bully others and make them feel small, so that it makes the person feel superior. This spirit is a reengage spirit and it must be dealt with when it rears its ugly head. It

must be chopped off at the root.

Building with Gaps

When helping to build a ministry or helping to keep the foundation stable. We want to build with no gaps. Building with gaps is a phrase that I use to help leadership know that what you don't know can hurt you. The scaffold is no good to the builder if there are gaps in the various levels that he is trying to build, and there can be no gaps when building. It doesn't matter if that building looks different, cracks can cause major damage in various parts of the foundation.

When you have leaders, who are out of place and not showing up on time or being disgruntled about a task that has been asked of them and they are complaining and just not very enthusiastic about the job they have been asked to do, this makes a very vivid point what we talked about earlier with the presumption spirit, with attitudes and movements in ministry that are not appropriate, it can cause others who are not in ministry who have no clear understanding of its structure begin to not question the leader but question the Under shepherd.

All fingers point to the shepherd when things go wrong at a church, whether they had anything to do with it or whether they were even there or not. Therefore, it's so important to have leaders who are mature in their own life. All the works that we do should always be done to the glory of God, and he gets full credit for it. When we complain watch out! Your building a hole in the scaffolding they may cause the rest of the scaffolding to crumble. The Bible tells us in *Eccles 5:1 Keep thy foot when thou goest to the house of God, and be ready to hear, then to give the sacrifice of fools: for they consider not that they do evil.*

So here we find that we are instructed to be careful with what we do in the house of God. This is not some random thing that we have to be careful of because we are leaders, this is for everyone! In other words, get your attitudes straight, fix that argument you had with your spouse before you step in and put on that fake front, you know how we like to do, we put up a front as if no one can see we are miserable and filled with hurt or anger. Then we are instructed to be more ready to hear.

The Message Bible says: enter to learn. We are not at church to get a feel-good message or a message that will comfort your flesh, we are there to learn. So, when we enter in, our hearts are fixed and our minds, eyes and ears are open to understanding. Glory! Truly when we have made those adjustments they become a part of who we are and then we can sing *Psalm 100:4 with confidence, enter into his gates with thanksgiving, And into His courts with praise. Be thankful to Him, and bless His name.*

Complaining will never do anything for anyone not even the complainer. Do you realize how detrimental it is to have leaders that complain?

Listen this is about leaders being mature enough to handle that which they said they were called too. Complaining disrupts unity; God hates the sin of division. The division spirit uses so many devices to infiltrate the camp (church) to cause disunity. It uses gossip, slander and it always, always finds the familiar spirit because they are attracted to each other. Also, manipulation is a big part of the spirit of division, this diabolical spirit doesn't care who it manipulates if it gets to do what it does best, it's a part in the bigger picture, it is very important as the secondary leaders that we don't allow complaining and division to be brought in the camp. This leads me to the next building scaffold.

We as leaders must understand one thing, everything that we do effect someone else. It's not to say you won't make mistakes or cross every T and dot every i; however we want to make sure that what we do for Christ is in order and reflects his glory and most of all over everything else done with a spirit of love.

There is nothing that we could ever do in God or for God and it is not or should never be done without the most important benefactor of love. This gets me to my next point. Our lifestyle is the key to get the more of Christ that we are yearning and asking for from him. We ask for the "more" of him in prayer in our worship, and we throw ourselves at the altar pleading for more. What if you haven't quite used the 'more" that's he's given you in your lifestyle? Our lives should reflect the life of Jesus Christ. Paul told the Corinthians that they were a living epistle, a witness to God's way of life. *2 Corinthians 3:3 Forasmuch as ye are manifestly declared to be the epistle of Christ ministered by us, written not with ink, but with the Spirit of the living God; not in tables of stone, but in fleshy tables of the heart.* I absolutely love that the tables of our heart. So, we move and interact in the spirit of love and the full unadulterated spirit of God. Leaders if at any time we are dealing with sensitive matters of families, marriage the whole totality of a human being we should have a lifestyle of praying a fasting so that we can hear from God. Yes, we all deal with something, but

74

our lives will be a direct representation of his glory or it won't be. We cannot afford to mess someone up and think well they will be ok when they go to another church... The things we do as leaders are detrimental. How can what I do as secondary leadership be all that important you ask? The people see you more than most before they see the Shepherd over that house. The shepherd is one person, but it's more than one in secondary leadership, so the sheep will see you more than they do the senior leader. Moses gave the orders, but in it was Aaron who told the people most times what Moses said to do! It's right in the book! *Exodus 4:28*

And Moses told Aaron all the words of

the LORD who had sent him, and all the signs which he had commanded him.

So here we find that Aaron was not in the dark about what God had told Moses to do as second in command he had an assignment, not only to the leader Moses but to God, to become a leader that does not hinder, a leader who is capable of following the commands of the Lord, a leader who was next in line to do the most important after Moses left off the scene and that is to carry the people over into the promise land. Secondary Leadership is detrimental to the success of the ministry. Someone must help keep the vision ever present before the people, and the leader. Do you realize that sometimes the leader must have a refreshed look at the vision why?

because ministry can pull on you that much and demand that much of your time, you can not only forget but things that happen in the ministry can move away from the original intent of what the vision was purposed to do! Building with gaps is so dangerous, because everyone loses in the end no one is benefitted when the scaffolding begins to shake and things become rocky, it is wobbling and too unstable to stand on and eventually falls and crumbles to the ground. There are no winners and souls are at stake and balanced on a limb, because leaders have failed to deal with the issues in its infancy stage, and now the problem or situation has matured beyond what we can actually handle, now in comes church hurt with all parties involved, and that situation has to find an immediate solution from the head leader while working with the secondary leaders and also the sheep have to be tended to, so as not to cause the repositions of the sheep going from one ministry to another hurt, without ever getting a solution to the situation.

In all I hope that you have gained some understanding and knowledge from what was written in this book, mostly it was basic surface level scraping to get to the main thing, which was serving with a servant's heart. We should continue to grow and become in Christ, it is a never-ending quest to learn more and more. So, as you begin your walk or just continue it, grow in grace, grow in peace and grow in love as you abound toward the main objective and that is the great commission.